P9-CFA-840

WITHDRAWN

MARIBYRNONG LIBRARY SERVICE

PETER POWERS™

and the
Rowdy Robot Raiders!

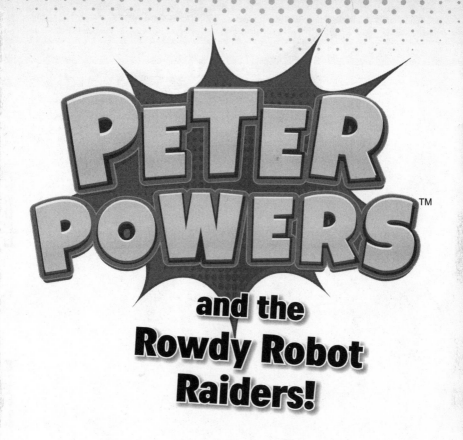

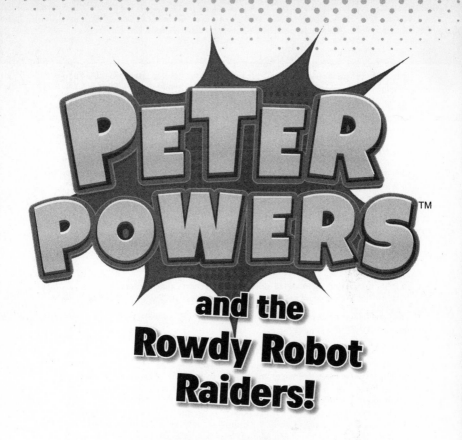

PETER POWERS™

and the Rowdy Robot Raiders!

**By Kent Clark
& Brandon T. Snider
Art by Dave Bardin**

Little, Brown and Company
New York Boston

This book is a work of fiction. Names, characters, places, and incidents are the product of the author's imagination or are used fictitiously. Any resemblance to actual events, locales, or persons, living or dead, is coincidental.

Copyright © 2016 by Hachette Book Group, Inc.
PETER POWERS is a trademark of Hachette Book Group.
Cover and interior art by Dave Bardin

All rights reserved. In accordance with the U.S. Copyright Act of 1976, the scanning, uploading, and electronic sharing of any part of this book without the permission of the publisher is unlawful piracy and theft of the author's intellectual property. If you would like to use material from the book (other than for review purposes), prior written permission must be obtained by contacting the publisher at permissions@hbgusa.com. Thank you for your support of the author's rights.

Little, Brown and Company

Hachette Book Group
1290 Avenue of the Americas, New York, NY 10104
Visit us at lb-kids.com

Little, Brown and Company is a division of Hachette Book Group, Inc.
The Little, Brown name and logo are trademarks of Hachette Book Group, Inc.

The publisher is not responsible for websites (or their content) that are not owned by the publisher.

First Edition: December 2016

Library of Congress Cataloging-in-Publication Data
Names: Clark, Kent. | Snider, Brandon T., author. | Bardin, Dave (Illustrator)
Title: Peter Powers and the rowdy robot raiders! / by Kent Clark &
    Brandon T. Snider ; art by Dave Bardin.
Description: First Edition. | Boston ; New York : Little, Brown and Company,
    2016. | Series: Peter Powers ; 2 | Summary: "When robots begin raiding the
    town, will Peter Powers and siblings be able to work together and help their
    parents?" —Provided by publisher.
Identifiers: LCCN 2016016354 | ISBN 9780316359412 (hardback) | ISBN
    9780316359399 (ebook) | ISBN 9780316359375 (library edition ebook)
Subjects: | CYAC: Superheroes—Fiction. | Ability—Fiction. | Family
    life—Fiction. | Robots—Fiction. | Humorous stories. | BISAC: JUVENILE
    FICTION / Action & Adventure / General. | JUVENILE FICTION / Humorous
    Stories. | JUVENILE FICTION / Readers / Chapter Books.
Classification: LCC PZ7.1.C594 Pe 2016 | DDC [Fic]—dc23
LC record available at https://lccn.loc.gov/2016016354

10 9 8 7 6 5 4 3 2 1

LSC-C

Printed in the United States of America

Contents

CHAPTER ONE
Backyard Barbecue

My name is Peter Powers. You've probably never heard of me. Most people haven't. But one day, I'm going to be the world's greatest superhero—or maybe the lamest. My super-power is super crummy. All I can do is make ice cubes with my fingers. *Not* cool.

Though I *did* defeat a supervillain! That's progress, right?

Even with the world's silliest superpower, I could still be a superhero. I mean, not anytime soon, but one day. Sure, I need

1

training and a code name and a costume and...Ugh. Definitely not anytime soon.

"Why the long face, son?" my dad said. My family was gathered in the backyard having a barbecue.

"I'm just bummed about my powers," I said.

"Don't be. When I was your age, all I could do was make my fingertips light up like birthday candles."

"Really?" I asked. Maybe there *was* hope for me.

"Yup. Now look at me!" My dad tossed some hot dogs on the grill, then held his hand over them. His hand made a big burst of flame, and in two seconds, the hot dogs were scorched! My dad loves to cook. He's also a full-fledged superhero who can control fire. It's pretty great.

"Those wieners need buns," Mom said, floating down from the sky with a plate of fresh bread. She's a superhero too, with the ability to fly. Super fast and super tough—I wish that was my power. "Fit like a glove," she said, grabbing the well-done hot dogs with the buns.

"Gavin, put your duplicates away and come eat!" Mom called out. Gavin is my older brother. He's definitely *not* a superhero, though he does have pretty rad powers. He can make exact duplicates of himself. Then there're two or four or even six versions of my brother running around being annoying. He's the worst.

"Hey, Felicia, can you put your phone down and join the family?" Dad asked. My younger sister, Felicia, rolled her eyes and acted like it was the end of the world. Since she couldn't text on her phone, she picked up a solid-steel beam and began bending it back and forth like it was a sheet of paper. You guessed it: She's super strong.

"OUCH!" Mom gasped. "I burned my finger on the grill."

I grabbed a towel and ran over. My fingers conjured up four perfect ice cubes. "Here, Mom, put this on it."

"Quick to the rescue," my dad noted. "Just like a hero."

I couldn't help but smile.

"Thanks, Peter," Mom said. "Hey, how did your class presentation go?"

And then my smile went away. It was such a simple question—with a not-so-simple answer. How could I tell my mom (a superhero!) that the presentation got totally messed up when Zack (the new kid— and BULLY—at school) totally destroyed my report (on purpose!)? I didn't want to admit that I was a big loser and an easy target for bullies.

"Greaaat!" I said, my voice cracking. I didn't feel like telling the truth in front of Gavin and Felicia. They would totally make fun of me.

"IT'S WIENER TIME!" Grandpa said, rolling his wheelchair into the backyard. My baby brother, Ben, sat on his lap. Grandpa Dale used to be a superhero, but now he mostly watches TV at home. He's a little crazy, but in the best possible way. For an old person, he's actually really cool. He's kind of my best friend. He did a 360 spin in his wheelchair, and Ben laughed.

"Dad! Be careful with Ben," Mom said, scooping up Ben and taking him into her arms. Ben has powers too, if you can believe it. He loves getting into trouble like any other baby, but he also can turn *invisible*, which makes him extra naughty. Grandpa likes getting into trouble and being naughty as well, though his powers are completely different. He has bird powers. He can sprout big wings and has super eyesight, or something like that.

"Time to stuff our gullets!" Grandpa cried out.

The entire Powers family sat down at the picnic table and ate. Family meals are the best. At least until Gavin or Felicia says, "I don't have enough ice in my drink. Refill, Peter?" Instead of going to the fridge, they make *me* put more ice in their cups.

Yup. That's what my powers are used for: I'm a walking ice cube tray.

CHAPTER TWO
Zack Attack

"What are we going to do about the Zack situation?" asked Chloe, throwing her lunch tray on the table. She was pretty stressed out about Zack, the new kid who also happened to be a total bully. "He stole my homework yesterday. He's not even in my class—he did it just to be mean."

"Zack took a candy bar right out of my hand," sniffed Sandro. My buddy loved food. And if there was one thing Sandro loved most, it was sweets. "It had peanut butter inside, Peter. PEANUT BUTTER!"

"What do you want *me* to do about it?" I asked. "He kicked me the other day when I was walking in the hallway. I tripped, dropped all my books, and fell into a trash can. Zack is a bully, case closed."

"Were you wearing a *Kick Me* sign?" Sandro asked. "Because if you *were*, that might be why he did it. Always check your back for signs, Peter. I do."

"I wasn't wearing a *Kick Me* sign," I said. "I was minding my own business."

"ZACK ATTACK!" someone suddenly screamed in my ear. Guess who it was? Zack stood behind me, laughing. He was

10

practically a giant. "Hey, Powers, there's something weird in your taters," he said. He stuck his finger up his nose, then shoved a big crusty booger right into my mashed potatoes. "Oh well. It's SNOT mine! HA-HA-HA!"

"That's pretty funny," giggled Sandro. Chloe nudged him in the ribs. "OUCH! I mean, that's pretty unfunny."

"Nice nuggets," Zack said, grabbing

the last two chicken nuggets on Sandro's tray and tossing them into his mouth. "*Mmmmmm. So nuggety. See you tomorrow, dorks.*" He walked away like he was the king of the cafeteria or something.

"Those were my LAST. TWO. NUGGETS," Sandro growled in disappointment. He was protective of all his food. "Peter, you need to *use your powers* and go get him! I can't live like this anymore!"

"Sandro, calm down," said Chloe. "They're just chicken nuggets."

"*JUST* chicken nuggets?" Sandro yelped. "You won't tell me to calm down when he steals *your* nuggets."

It was one thing for Zack to pick on me.

But it was another thing for him to pick on my friends. I felt myself getting madder and madder. I felt like I was going to burst into flames—which is kind of funny since my power is creating ice cubes.

Suddenly, I shouted, "HEY, ZACK!"

Zack paused and turned around. The look on his face told me he wasn't expecting to be yelled at by me or anyone else.

"Can I help you with something, Powers?" Zack shouted from halfway across the cafeteria. The entire lunchroom was watching.

I gulped. What was I thinking?!

"*Don't*, Peter," Chloe whispered. "It's not worth it. Don't use your powers."

"I have to! He can't keep doing this," I whispered back. "We have to teach that bully a lesson."

"Think it through, Peter. If you use your powers to go after Zack now, you'll get in trouble *and* blow your secret identity. Then your mom will ground you. And if you're grounded, you won't get to come see *Vampire Boat* with us next week."

I'd been looking forward to seeing the latest *Vampire Boat* movie with my friends for months.

"It's vampires on a boat! There's no way you want to miss it," said Sandro.

"Sandro, *you're* the one who just told me to get Zack," I whispered.

"I know, I know. But then I thought it through," said Sandro. "Plus, Chloe's right. You shouldn't use your powers in public."

"*Grrr*," I growled. Zack was staring at me, and the whole lunchroom was waiting.

My friends were right. I couldn't use my powers to hurt him. That's not what a hero

would do. Would I love to shove an ice cube right up his nose? Absolutely. But not today.

"Well, Powers?" Zack snorted. "You got something to say, say it."

"Um...I really...uh...like your shirt?" I said awkwardly.

Zack looked at me like I was the weirdest kid in the world. Maybe I was. Chloe nodded, and Sandro gave me a weak thumbs-up. What was I going to do? Besides becoming the most embarrassing excuse for a superhero-in-training ever.

CHAPTER THREE
Family Meeting

"FAMILY MEETING!" Mom yelled. She was so loud that the house shook. I slowly made my way down the stairs as Gavin ran by, pushing me aside.

"First one here!" Gavin said. He sat on the couch and smiled proudly. Felicia took her time getting there. Once we were all seated, Mom stared at Gavin like she wasn't buying what he was selling.

"GAVIN! Get down here this instant!"

Mom shouted. "I know you're up there playing video games. Do you think I can't tell the difference between my son and one of his duplicates?" The Gavin copy made a frowny face, got up from the couch, and ran outside. The *real* Gavin whined all the way down the stairs. Nothing gets by Mom.

"Listen up, everyone. Some weird stuff is happening in Boulder City, so Mom and I are heading out tonight to go undercover," Dad said.

Undercover! That's so exciting. I wish I could go undercover. I'd put on a fake mustache and a top hat and talk with a funny accent. Or something. That's what going undercover is all about, right?

"What's the situation?" I asked.

"Cars are being stripped of parts. Scrap-yards are being pillaged. An entire bank vault was even stolen—but the money was left behind," Mom said, shaking her head. "Someone is stealing metal all over the city, but we don't know who or why."

"But we're going to find out," Dad said. "It might be a late night, so we need you three to keep an eye on your baby brother."

"WHAT?" shouted Felicia. She crushed the soda can in her hand so hard, it looked like a tiny piece of metal string.

"But babies are weird!" moaned Gavin. "Why can't Grandpa watch him?"

"Grandpa has plans tonight. He's going to play bingo with his friends," Mom said. "But all of you are old enough to work together and help out. I want you to promise me that you will try your hardest to respect one another, follow the rules, and make sure your brother doesn't disappear forever. Can you do that? Please, we need you to work as a team."

"I'm already on a team," proclaimed Gavin. "It's called the Gavin Squad. All Gavins, all the time. We're pretty popular on the Internet."

"I am NOT changing a single diaper. I called it. No backsies!" Felicia declared.

"We can do it!" I said enthusiastically. "We'll work together! As a team!" I figured a positive approach might inspire my siblings. Instead, they both rolled their eyes at me.

Mom and Dad looked at the three of us, worried.

"It'll be fine," I said. "What could *possibly* go wrong?"

CHAPTER FOUR
Babysit Fail

"*Geeeeee!*" my little brother cooed. Ben sat on my lap, watching his favorite show, *Mr. Picklekins*. The first rule of babysitting a baby who can turn invisible is to keep him close to you at all times.

So far, the night was going pretty smoothly. Felicia was doing her homework. And Ben was clapping at his TV show. Not an ounce of drama to be had.

"Can you change the channel, Peter? *Mr. Picklekins* is awful. I can't listen to it and do my homework," complained Felicia. "Who cares about a talking-pickle police officer? Let's watch *Teen Court*."

"*Mr. Picklekins is* awful, but Ben loves it," I said. "We need to keep him happy so he doesn't turn invisible on us."

"He's just a baby," Felicia moaned. "He doesn't care." She snatched the remote and changed the channel.

"*PICKLE!*" Ben cried.

I snatched the remote, changing it back. "Just let him watch it," I argued.

Felicia grabbed the remote. I grabbed it back. We started to fight over it.

"I want to watch *Teen Court!*" my sister said snippishly.

"Let Ben watch his show!" I snapped.

"PICKLE!!" Ben screamed.

Felicia was stronger than me, but I wouldn't let go of the remote. I was so angry that my ice power accidentally went off. In an instant, I froze the remote control in a block of solid ice.

"Peter! You flash-froze the remote!" Felicia shouted.

"I didn't even know I could do that," I said. "Cool."

"*Not* cool," Felicia said, crushing the iced remote in her hand into a million pieces. "I'm leaving. I'll watch *Teen Court* at Rachel's house."

"Mom and Dad said we were *all* supposed to watch Ben!" I growled.

"He's a baby. You and Gavin can handle him," Felicia argued.

"Where *is* Gavin?" I asked. "Gavin! Get down here and help!"

"What do you want?!" Gavin shouted, appearing at the top of the stairs.

"We need your help watching Ben," I
said.

"Where is he?" Gavin asked.

I looked around the living room. Ben
was nowhere in sight.

"BEN IS GONE!" I shouted.

"I told you not to sit him down," Felicia
yelled at me.

"No, you didn't! And this isn't my fault! You're the one who tried to shut off his favorite show!" I yelled back.

"Let me handle this," said Gavin. He used his power to create five...eight... no, twelve copies of himself! "There's no way he's getting out of the house now!" all twelve Gavins said at the same time.

"But now there's nowhere to move!" Felicia squirmed. "*Ow!* You stepped on my toe!"

"Sorry!" all twelve Gavins shouted at once.

"I think I feel him crawling through my legs!" shouted Gavin #3.

"He just crawled past me!" yelled Gavin #7.

"I'm hungry!" whined Gavin #12.

There was too much happening all at once. Ben was *lost*, Felicia was *freaking out*, there were *so many* Gavins in the living room knocking over *everything*, and I was about to lose my mind.

CRASH! Gavin #4 knocked over the lamp.

SMASH! Gavin #11 bumped into Mom's favorite vase. It shattered when it hit the ground.

CRASH! SMASH! SPLASH! Gavin #9 fell, pulling the tablecloth—and dinner and a pitcher of iced tea—with him. Plates broke. Glasses cracked. The iced tea went everywhere.

"I think Ben bit my leg!" yelped Gavin #2. Sure enough, Ben appeared again, chomping on Gavin #2's leg and giggling. I scooped my baby brother up into my arms as the real Gavin absorbed all of his duplicates back into himself.

The house was a total wreck!

Of course *that's* when my parents

walked in the door.

CHAPTER FIVE
Bully Blues

It was almost lunchtime, but Chloe and Sandro were nowhere to be found. As I closed my locker, the giant bully turned the corner. "Hey, Powers," Zack said. "What's up?"

What's up? I thought. What's up is that I am *stressed*. Babysitting Ben was a disaster. When my parents got home and saw the huge mess that all the Gavins made, they were the *opposite* of happy. No one got grounded, thankfully. But Mom said she was disappointed in all of us. Somehow, that was worse than her being mad.

Of course, I didn't say any of that to the big bully. Instead I said, "Just waiting for my friends."

"What's that supposed to mean?" Zack sneered, leaning down and whispering directly into my ear. "You think I don't have any friends?"

I gulped. I could toss some ice cubes at him, but (a) I didn't think that would be helpful, and (b) my parents would ground me big-time if I used my powers at school.

"I'm sure you have friends," I said. "Lots of them. Like, hundreds. No...er...I mean, thousands!"

Zack's eyes bulged out of his head. "You being *sarcastic*?!" The big kid picked me up by my shoulders and hung me on the outside of my locker. I was wearing my favorite hoodie. If it ripped, I was going to be really mad. I felt a tingle in my fingers. My cold power was warming up. I took a deep breath and shut it off. No powers at school. No matter what. I knew that.

"Don't mess with me again, Powers,"
growled Zack. "You've been warned."

He walked away in a huff as I spotted
Chloe and Sandro coming from the other
direction. "Hey, friends!" I said. "Mind
helping me down before someone else
sees me?"

After Chloe and Sandro helped me
down, I noticed Sandro's black eye. "What
happened?"

"Zack kind of, sort of punched me in the
face," Sandro said.

"And he stole my homework again,"
Chloe said.

"That's it!" I said, gritting my teeth.
"This bullying has to stop! No one is going

to push my friends around. Not Zack, not anyone! This means WAR!"

My heart was racing. I punched my fists together, and they started to ice up.

"Peter, wait," said Chloe. "Shut down your powers! I don't know why Zack is so mean. Maybe he isn't adjusting to the new school? Maybe he's around a lot of anger at home? I don't have all the answers, but I do know it's not worth fighting him. That'll just make him madder—it won't solve *the problem*. There *has* to be a better way, right?"

I really wanted to go give Zack a piece of my mind, but Chloe had a point.

"We'll think of something," said Sandro, as he began shivering. "*Brrrrr*, did it get chilly in here all of a sudden? Peter, is that *you*?"

"Um, yeah?" I said. "I guess when I get mad, my cold power gets stronger."

Sandro's frown reversed direction. "Peter, that's amazing! You're going to be the world's most awesome superhero one day."

"You think?" I asked.

"Well," Sandro said, "only if you can survive school bullies first."

CHAPTER SIX
Team Errands

"Here is a list of errands around town," Dad said to me, Gavin, and Felicia. "These are all things that you need to complete. *Together*. Any questions?"

"Why are you making us do this *together*?" asked Felicia in the most dramatic way possible. "Wouldn't it be easier to order this stuff online?"

"It might be easier, sure, but ease isn't the issue," Mom said. "We want the three of you to find ways to *work together*. This family is a *team*. No weak links." She added, "Don't let us down." Our parents shoved us out the front door.

Gavin grinned mischievously. I could already tell what he was thinking.

"Don't sweat it. My duplicates can do this stuff, and we can go watch a movie or something," he said, smirking. I knew he was going to say that.

So did Mom, who swung the front door open to deliver a final message: "Gavin, if you make even a single duplicate, you're grounded. No powers. At all. From any of you."

"No shortcuts!" Dad added. He shut the door again.

"Thanks, Peter," said Felicia.

"What did *I* do?" I asked.

"We have to do all these team-building exercises because *you* don't know how to babysit the right way," Felicia snapped.

"All *three of us* were supposed to babysit!" I countered. "And it was Gavin's duplicates who made the mess!"

"Whatever." Gavin shrugged.

"Dad is right. We do need to learn how to work as a team," I said. My brother and sister weren't having it.

Felicia tore the list of errands into three pieces of paper. She took one part and gave the other parts to me and Gavin. "We'll divide and conquer. Meet you back here in an hour," she said, grabbing her bike and taking off.

"You're missing the point!" I pleaded as she rode away. But she didn't stop.

"I like her plan. Better than having to spend the whole day with you," said Gavin. He took off down the street on his bike.

"Where are you going?" I shouted.

"Anywhere but here!" he yelled back, seemingly without a care in the world.

I was furious. I didn't want to get grounded because my brother and sister wouldn't cooperate. Still, at the very least, I needed to run my share of the errands. Maybe we wouldn't get caught, and everything would be fine.

I hopped on my bike and rode toward my first errand: picking up a box at the post office. After locking up my bike, I went inside. When I came out, I noticed that some of the cars parked in front of the building looked wrong. Probably because they were just tires and seats. Everything else had been stripped away.

"Must be a bad neighborhood," I said to myself. "I'm glad no one thought to steal— *HEY, THAT'S MY BIKE!*"

An army of robot raiders had sawed through the bike chain with lasers! They were stealing my bike. I ran after them. "Put that down!" I shouted, raising my hands. Two dozen ice cubes shot out of my fingers.

Some of the robots stopped and turned. They started walking toward me. "Uh-oh," I said out loud. "Bad move."

Suddenly, I was surrounded.

CHAPTER SEVEN
The Robot Raiders

"You're the thieves who have been stealing all the metal, aren't you?" I asked the robots surrounding me. "Why are you raiding the town?"

The robots didn't say anything. Instead they *buzzed* and *clicked* as they walked closer.

"Um, I'm not really a fan of fighting," I said. "So it'd be great if we could just call it a day and all go home. How's that sound?"

The robot raiders were spread out across the parking lot. There were countless robots everywhere. I found myself wishing I had cool magnet powers. A few people were running and screaming. The robots weren't chasing them, though. They only wanted the metal.

I pulled out my keys and held them up in the air with a jingle. All the robots

became alert—the same way a dog does when you wave a stick in front of it.

"Wanna play fetch?" I asked. I tossed the keys. All the robots chased after them.

Suddenly, I heard Gavin and Felicia screaming in the distance. They were pedaling their bikes down the road. More robot raiders were clunking along after them too.

"*GAAAAHHHH!*" cried Gavin. "Robots! Robots chasing me! Robots want to hurt me!"

"Metal-eating monsters!" Felicia added with a scream.

"They just want your bikes!" I shouted. "Hop off your bikes. They won't hurt you!"

"No way!" Gavin said, pedaling toward me. "I love this bike!"

"I'm not giving them my bike either!" Felicia growled. As my brother and sister arrived at my side, they dropped their bikes and hopped behind me. "Ice them up, brother!"

"You know my powers don't work like that!" I shouted, as an army of robot raiders surrounded us.

"Nice robots," I said as politely as I could,

raising my hands. "Don't attack. Be nice to humans."

The metal monsters looked at me like I was crazy. Gavin and Felicia must have forgotten they had superpowers—because they hid behind me like a couple of scaredy-cats. What was I supposed to do?!

"Get away from my kids!" Dad shouted, blasting the metal-raiding robots with a huge wall of flame. The rest of the robots scattered.

"Are you all okay?" Dad asked. We nodded yes.

"Good. Stay put. I'll be right back." He chased after the robots, using his fire power to corral them.

Then the ground shook. Four gorilla-sized robots stomped toward us. They raised their hands and shot lasers at Dad. Suddenly, Mom flew out of the sky and rammed into the robots, knocking them down like bowling pins.

"Honey, keep your eyes open!" Mom shouted.

Dad looked annoyed. "I *did* have my eyes open, dear." It seemed like they'd both had a long day. There were a few

robots left. Dad used his flames to melt them in place.

When the battle was over, my family stood in the middle of a parking lot full of melted robots and car-less tires. My parents seemed frustrated. "You *didn't* stay together, did you?" Mom asked.

"Um...about that," Gavin began. Felicia looked at her hands, unable to make eye contact with our parents.

Dad sighed. All Mom said was, "You need to learn to work together." Then she gave Dad a look. I knew that look. She was disappointed. As usual, that was worse than getting in trouble.

CHAPTER EIGHT
Lectures for Everyone

Over the next few days, Mom and Dad battled robot after robot after robot. Some were small robots; some were huge robots. But all of them were trying to steal metal from around Boulder City. And no matter how many robot raiders Mom and Dad stopped, more kept coming.

"What a week," Dad sighed as he came in. His costume was in tatters.

"Tell me about it," Mom said. She didn't look so hot either.

They looked exhausted. Part of me was grateful that they had been too busy to come down on me, Gavin, and Felicia for not working together. To try to make up for things, I had cleaned the whole house from top to bottom. It was nothing less than spotless. (I may hate cleaning, but I take pride in my work.) But Mom and Dad were so tired, they didn't even notice. After they came in and pulled off their boots, they both collapsed on the couch.

"Honey, did you not see that robot come up beside me?" asked Dad.

"I *did* see it," Mom replied tersely. "And I knew you'd handle it."

"I was busy melting all those other

raiding robots. That sneaky one almost took me out," Dad said, shaking his head.

"Well, I was busy grabbing robots and flying them into space. I guess I expected you to rise to the occasion," Mom sniped. My parents don't fight, but they can have some very tense conversations from time to time.

"I need a shower and a nap. Especially if we're going to go back out there after dinner," Mom said. She kissed me on the cheek and went upstairs. The rest of us sat quietly for a moment. Silence can be weird sometimes, even with your family.

"If those robots think they're going to take the *TV*, they've got another think coming!" Grandpa said, rolling into the room in his wheelchair. He made fists and boxed at the air. "I'll give 'em the old one-two!"

"I'm with Grandpa," Gavin said, boxing at the air too.

"Don't make fun of me, you whipper-snapper!" Grandpa said. He ran over Gavin's toe with his wheel. "If the robots do come, the only one who stands a chance is *Peter*. Peter will have to save the whole family."

"I think you've got me confused with someone else," I said.

"Seriously," Felicia said. "The only one who stands a real chance is me."

"You didn't seem to think that the other

day when you hid behind me," I whispered.

"All three of you have to learn *teamwork* first," Dad said, giving Grandpa a knowing glance. Gavin and Felicia looked down. I think they were embarrassed.

"So do *you*, Mister!" Grandpa said to Dad. "From what I saw, you and that daughter of mine could use a refresher class in teamwork."

"How would you know?" Dad said. "You weren't there!"

"Wasn't I?" Grandpa asked, flapping his wings at Dad. "Sometimes I like to stretch my wings, and when I do, I see everything. They used to call me Eagle-Eye Pete in the old days."

"But your name is Dale," I said.

"So?" Grandpa shrugged, then started laughing and wheeled away.

"Touché!" I said jokingly. I'd heard people say that on TV, after they call someone out about something. I didn't know what it meant, but it sounded cool. Dad looked at me with a raised eyebrow.

"Do you even know what that word means, Peter?" he asked.

"Nope," I said.

Dad patted me on the head. "Grandpa Dale makes a good point. We *all* have lots of stuff to think about, and still more to learn. Go grab some bowls and some spoons. Meet me in the dining room for ice cream." Gavin and Felicia took off running. Ice cream can have that effect on people.

"You're the *best*, Dad," I said.

"I'm not," Dad replied, "but I try my hardest, and that's what counts. Teamwork isn't always easy, but in the long run, it makes things better. Remember that, will you?"

"I promise," I said.

CHAPTER NINE
Missing Parents

"WHERE ARE THEY?" Felicia asked the next afternoon. Sometimes she acts like things are a big deal when they are totally not a big deal. It makes her feel cool. But this time, I thought her worries were justified. I was worried too—our parents were missing.

Yesterday, Mom and Dad came home, rested up, and then went out again. Battling robots overnight was one thing, but they still weren't back. No matter who they fought, they were always home by breakfast time. And when they were held up, they always sent a text to let us know everything was okay. But not today. It was late afternoon, and none of us had heard from them.

"Mom and Dad were arguing last night," Gavin said. "Do you think they broke up?"

"Are you insane?" snapped Felicia. "Our parents had a disagreement—that doesn't mean they're getting a divorce." She looked at me. "Right, Peter?"

Gulp. I'm the middle kid. Why were they looking to me for advice?!

I tried to say something positive and reassuring. "Uh...well, the three of us argue all the time and we're not getting a divorce. Oh, wait, that doesn't make any sense. Um, Mom and Dad are adults, and adults don't always see eye to eye, so maybe they needed some time apart. No, that's not what I meant either...." I was mucking this up. Trying to sound wise was hard.

"*True* teamwork is about *listening* to your partner and *communicating*," I said. That was it. That made sense. Didn't it?

"Huh?" grumbled Gavin. "I wasn't paying attention."

No surprise there.

"I can't stand this. I need to relax," Felicia said, flipping on the television. "A little *Teen Court* should ease my mind."

Ugh. That show is so dumb. Anything but *Teen Court*, I thought. The TV teens were about to have a sappy, kissy-face moment. I was about to puke when the channel turned to static.

No *Teen Court*? This was my lucky day!

Then the static on the TV screen changed into live footage of someone. A new face appeared—one much worse than kissy-face teens on *Teen Court*. He looked like a regular guy, except instead of hair, you could see his brain. And it was huge! Now I was *really* going to puke!

"Hello, Boulder City! You may be asking yourself, 'Who is that beautiful man with

the big brain on my TV screen right now?'
Well, it's me, your soon-to-be ruler! But you
can call me *THE NEFARIOUS BRAIN!*"

"Uh-oh," I said. "Looks like a new supervillain is in town."

"You've no doubt seen my robot raiders around town," he continued. "They've been raiding your city for all kinds of shiny steel and sleek metal. *Why, you ask? Because I needed the materials to make THAT!"

The TV revealed a giant robot. And when I say giant, I mean a *forty-foot-tall* giant!

"I call him *Ginormo the Megabot.* And Ginormo is here to drink oil and kick butt. And he's all out of oil!" The Nefarious Brain paused for a moment. "Did I say that right? It doesn't matter. That's Ginormo's catchphrase. You'll be seeing it on T-shirts, mugs, buttons, you name it."

"That guy's robots stole my bike!" I

growled. Gavin and Felicia were glued to their seats, but seeing this weirdo on TV made me want to go teach him a lesson he'd never forget. Of course, what was I going to do? Offer him an ice-cold drink? Let's face it: My powers were no match for a giant robot.

The Nefarious Brain turned toward the camera. "You may be asking yourself, where are Boulder City's two most famous heroes?"

"Yeah! Where are Mom and Dad?" Gavin said. "Shouldn't they be destroying this Brain dude *and* his dumb mega-toaster?"

They *should* have been. The fact that they weren't worried me.

The Brain spoke again. "They're about to appear right before your very eyes! Look up!"

"Yes! Here comes *Team Powers* to save the day!" Gavin cheered.

"C'mon, Mom and Dad!" Felicia said. "Show this guy what's up!"

I was too nervous to cheer. I suspected the worst.

The Nefarious Brain pulled a remote control out of his pocket. (It looked just like a TV remote.) He pressed a series of buttons. Then Ginormo the Megabot's chest panel opened up. Inside, Mom and Dad were locked up and plugged in.

"Your precious superheroes are nothing more than *batteries* now," the Nefarious Brain said with a laugh. "I'm using your heroes to power my giant robot."

CHAPTER TEN
Sibling Rivalry

"Let's go!" said Gavin, tossing soda cans into his backpack. "We'll need lots of caffeine and sugar for this takedown." He devoured a candy bar.

"How do you know where they are?" I asked.

"There's a forty-foot-tall robot standing next to the highway," Felicia said. See? That's why Felicia is considered the smart one in the family. "You stay here and watch Ben and Grandpa."

"Where are you going?" I asked. I knew the answer, but I could hardly believe it.

"Where do you think, squirt?" Gavin said. "We're gonna take down the Nerd-burger Brain and his lame robot raiders. Once we save our parents, they'll never ground us again."

"This is a terrible idea," I said. "Neither of you has any idea what you're doing!"

"Sure I do. I'm going to make so many duplicates of myself that that lame Ginormo won't know what hit him," bragged Gavin.

It wasn't a *bad* plan, but a thousand things could go wrong. "Time for Peter Powers and his child-sized brain to swing into action," I mumbled to myself. Wait, that didn't sound right.

"If one of your duplicates gets hurt, do you feel it too?" I asked.

"Yeah. Why?" Gavin said, giving me an angry look.

"Then Ginormo could take you out in one second flat."

"Don't worry, I'm strong enough to take down that stupid robot," said Felicia, folding her arms like she was in charge all of a sudden.

"You're super strong, but are you invulnerable?" I asked.

"I don't know. Why?" Felicia asked, concerned.

"The Nefarious Brain has a whole team of robot raiders—and some have lasers. If you aren't laser-proof, I'm not sure it's a good idea for you to run in there alone."

My siblings both stared at me the way they always stare at me—like I'm an alien and they can't understand the words coming out of my mouth.

"We're still going," Felicia said.

"Yeah," Gavin said, strapping his backpack on. "But I should be in charge. I'm the *oldest*, and I know what's best. It's what Dad would want."

"No way. I'm the *smartest*, so I know what's best. I should be in charge. That's what Mom would want," countered Felicia.

These two were driving me crazy. Was it possible that they never listened to our parents?! I couldn't hold my tongue any longer. I shouted, *"YOU KNOW WHAT MOM AND DAD WOULD REALLY WANT? FOR US TO WORK TOGETHER!"*

There was some more staring—but this time they knew *exactly* what I was talking about. Gavin and Felicia looked at each other and stood up. It seemed like they were finally ready for some teamwork. I think I finally might've changed their minds.

"WHATEVER," Felicia said, storming out the door.

"Yeah, whatever," Gavin said, following Felicia.

So maybe I didn't change their minds. But I wasn't giving up on teamwork just yet. I wasn't going to let my dumb brother and overconfident sister go fight a supervillain alone. "Hold on, you two. I'm going."

CHAPTER ELEVEN
Break-In

"Grandpa!!!" I yelled, running into his hobby room—that's what he calls the garage. He was watching TV—which is what he calls a hobby.

"Where's little Ben?" I asked. "I thought he was with you."

"*Shhh*. He's right here, Peter," Grandpa whispered, rocking his arms back and forth. He looked down at his empty arms and began to coo. "Ben is sleeping like a good invisible baby. Yes, you are, aren't you, Grandpa's invisible boy?"

Felicia and Gavin were waiting outside. We were about to go rescue our parents, but first I needed to make sure Grandpa had things under control while we were gone. It looked like he did.

That is, until a very *visible* Ben crawled in from the other room, bright-eyed and giggly, pretending to be a dog.

"Uh, Grandpa?" I said. "That's Ben over there."

Grandpa looked at Ben, then down at

his empty arms. "If *that's* Ben, then who is *this*?" he asked. The moment hung in the air, until Grandpa cracked up and began laughing mischievously. "*Hee-hee-hee!* Peter, the look on your face always makes it worthwhile. Don't worry about us," he said. "We're going to go play in the dryer!"

"Grandpa, can you be serious for one second, please?" I asked. "This is important."

"I know it is, Peter," Grandpa said. His tone became serious. "I've got everything under control here. You go take care of business, but be careful. Keep an eye on your siblings. Watch their backs—and yours. And bring your parents home."

"How did you—" I started.

"Know?" Grandpa smiled. "Flying and seeing aren't my only superpowers. And when you're out there, remember"— Grandpa's tone turned very serious—"to pick up a bag of Dr. Snackington's Loaded Pretzel Skins. They're delicious."

"If I survive, I'll see what I can do," I said.

I ran outside to find Gavin and Felicia waiting impatiently. "You're as slow as melting ice!" Gavin said. "Come on, let's go."

He hopped on his bike. Felicia hopped on her bike. And I—ugh, this is *so embarrassing*. I used Felicia's old bike. It was pink and had a flower basket on the front. Not exactly how I envisioned traveling to defeat my first giant robot.

The Nefarious Brain may have had an oversize brain, but he didn't seem so smart to me. His *not*-so-secret hideout was a warehouse guarded by a forty-foot-tall giant robot. It was like a sign saying, "Come get me, good guys!"

Of course, once me and my siblings arrived, I realized why. There were a hundred robots guarding the warehouse.

Making sure we weren't seen, we hid our bikes behind a wooden fence. I scanned the area for trouble.

"Most of the robot raiders are standing

guard over there," I noted. "That must be where the Brain is hiding. If we can get to him, we can stop him!"

"Are you kidding?" Gavin sneered. "How are we supposed to get past all those robot guards?"

"Let me smash 'em all," Felicia said.

"No, not yet," I said. "Gavin, create a couple of copies and have them run in the other direction. The guards will chase them and we'll be free to go in. But whatever happens, we stick *together*."

"That's exactly what I was thinking," Gavin said. *Yeah, sure*, I thought.

He used his power, and Gavin #2

and Gavin #3 started running. They did
the chicken dance to get the robots'
attention, then took off running in another
direction.

"WE ARE INSULTED BY YOUR STRANGE
DANCE, HUMANS. WE WILL CATCH YOU

NOW," the robot guards said together. They chased after the Gavin copies.

"Now, Felicia, you rip the door off its hinges, but watch out for—"

Before she heard my plan, my sister ran ahead. She tripped the security alarm I was about to warn her about.

A siren went off, and a giant squidlike robot climbed out of the ground. One of its enormous metal tentacles grabbed Felicia. Then it caught me and Gavin. Its tentacles wrapped around us like metal boa constrictors. Its vise was so tight, we couldn't use our powers.

"Intruders must be taken to MASTER," the robot squid said, carrying us away. It took us inside the giant warehouse and dropped each of us into our own metal cage. It flipped a switch, and the bars became electrified.

A metal elevator lowered itself into the room. When the doors opened, we were all

shocked. It was the Nefarious Brain! But he wasn't exactly what we'd expected.

CHAPTER TWELVE
Time for a Plan

"YOU'RE TINY!" Gavin laughed at the supervillain.

It was true. The man from the TV had seemed so terrifying. But the real Nefarious Brain was on the small side. He was barely three feet tall. He walked past our cages and took a seat at his desk. He began typing away at his computer, trying to ignore Gavin.

"How old are you? You look like a little kid!"

"I am twenty-eight years old," the Brain mumbled. "I'm just small for my age."

"Twenty-eight? More like two feet eight inches tall!" Gavin laughed.

"Size doesn't matter. You're exceptionally tall, but you're the one locked in a cage while I'm out here building the world's biggest robot. I don't need superpowers for that, just a big brain. Do the math on that one—if you even know *how* to do math."

"He doesn't!" I said. That got the Brain's attention. "Hi, uh...Mr. Brain? Gavin is a total tool, I know. And I know how you feel—about size, I mean. I'm the shortest kid in my class. I may have superpowers, but they're totally crummy."

The Nefarious Brain studied me. I tried to smile.

"So, um, how did you become an evil genius?" I asked.

The Nefarious Brain grinned from ear to ear. The one thing you can always count on with bad guys is that they love to talk about themselves. Sometimes they even give away their entire plan.

"Well, you know, I didn't *intend* to become an evil genius. I just wanted to build robots to do my evil errands. Now I've got an entire army of robot raiders," he said. "The good thing about robots is that they all follow a single command. When an army *works together*, it can accomplish anything—even conquering the world." The Brain scratched his exposed brain. "I should put that on a T-shirt."

"Working together," I said, nodding to Gavin and Felicia. "How fun that must be for you and your robot army."

"Yeah, they're great. Without my metal minions, I could never have raided all the supplies to make Ginormo myself," said the Brain. "You know what they say—it takes an army to build a giant. We're a well-oiled machine like that. Well, *they* are well-oiled machines. I'm oily in a *different* way."

Ew, I thought.

The Nefarious Brain kept typing away at his computer. "You know, you guys might have stood a better chance if you'd worked together."

"Thank you!" I sighed. Normally I didn't like agreeing with supervillains, but this one was pretty smart.

"Now, if you don't mind, I have work to do," the Brain said. "Once Ginormo is completed, I plan on using him to take over the city—and then the world!"

The Nefarious Brain pressed a button. A glowing energy shield appeared around the villain. He put on his headphones and went back to doing computer stuff— and scratching his exposed brain. Double ew. He pulled a remote out of his pocket and placed it next to his computer.

I recognized the remote from the TV. It controlled Ginormo.

A plan started forming in my head.

"Are you two willing to listen to me and *work together?*" I whispered to Gavin and Felicia. "I need you two to promise to work *with* me, not *against* me. This is make or break time, people!" I'd heard that last line in a movie.

"We'll do whatever you say, just get us out of here," Gavin replied in the loudest whisper ever. So dumb.

"Fine, yes," Felicia hissed.

"All right! We're in business. Gavin, reach through the bars without touching them, so you don't get shocked. Then

make a copy of yourself *outside* the cage.
Have him press the button that releases
us. Then, Felicia, you smash that shield
around the Brain. Then leave the rest
to me."

The Nefarious Brain was so busy
tinkering with his computer, he wasn't
paying attention to us. Gavin took a

deep breath and created a copy. Gavin #2 tiptoed over to the big red button that controlled our cages. He pressed it and we were free.

Felicia grabbed hold of the shield. She pulled with all her might. The whole room started to shake. Felicia ripped the shield open, and the generator exploded.

"What are you doing?!" the Brain shouted. "Get back in your cages!"

"I don't think so." Felicia raised her fist.

"Don't hit me!" he said, cowering— except he wasn't cowering, he was reaching for the alarm. A siren blared!

"Robot raiders—*help your master!*" he shouted into his remote. His army of robots

swarmed the room. Gavin multiplied, and Felicia started hitting.

I had to act fast. The Brain's remote controlled his robots—I had to steal it from him. I leaped across his desk and grabbed it. "Let go!" he shouted.

"No, you let go!" I yelled.

The struggle for the remote reminded me of the same struggle over the TV remote last week with Felicia. I didn't give up then, and I wouldn't give up now. Wait, I thought. That's it! That's what I needed to do!

I let my anger wash through me and focused all of it into my ice energy. "Chill out!" I said. The remote control flash-froze, turning into a big block of ice.

"NOOOOOO!" the Brain cried.

The Nefarious Brain couldn't control his robots without the remote. The lights went out in the eyes of every single robot raider in the warehouse, and they stopped moving.

"My precious robots! My precious plans! You ruined everything!"

Felicia picked up the Brain and put him in one of the cages. Then a bunch of Gavins helped me peel the front panel off Ginormo. Inside, Mom and Dad were still locked up—that is, until Felicia ripped them free with her super strength.

Our parents gave us a group hug. The Nefarious Brain had been taken down, the robot raiders were out of commission, and the Powers family was reunited.

CHAPTER THIRTEEN
In Trouble...Again!

Gavin, Felicia, and I were lined up on the couch as Dad paced in front of us. Mom was standing with her arms folded, looking stern. These were not good signs.

"Um, shouldn't we be getting rewarded?" Gavin asked.

"Maybe a cash prize?" Felicia asked.

Our parents looked angry. We saved the day—why were we in trouble? We were totally confused.

"We are very proud of you three,"

Mom began. She was talking slowly, which meant she was selecting her words carefully. She only did that when she was really mad. "We don't expect you to make the right choices all the time, but we do expect you to be more responsible."

Dad stopped pacing. "Mom and I appreciate that you wanted to save us. That was very sweet of you. But we told you to stay put here at the house for your own safety. You didn't do that."

"We used *teamwork*, though," Gavin said. His eyes became bright, as if the thought had just occurred to him.

"You *did* use teamwork," Dad said.

"That's correct. And I'm glad. But you put yourselves in danger."

"Peter is the one who told us to work together," Felicia said. "If anyone's in trouble, it should be him."

"What?!" I moaned. "Thanks for turning on me!"

Felicia shrugged.

"All of you disobeyed," Dad said.

"Which means all of you are in trouble," Mom added.

Then, at the same time, Mom and Dad said, "You're all grounded."

Oh well. At least it wasn't just me this time.

"And Grandpa Dale is grounded as well," Dad said. A second later, a loud crash echoed throughout the house. It came from Grandpa's room.

"Say what now?" asked Grandpa, wheeling into the living room like a race-car. "How can *I* be grounded? I didn't do anything wrong."

"You let the kids go fight a supervillain alone," Mom growled. "Again!"

"They weren't alone. I had my super eagle-eye vision on them the entire time. I never let 'em out of my sight!"

Dad gave Grandpa a look—the not-happy kind he usually gives us. "You

cannot let the kids go off to battle," said
Dad. "We keep going through this."

Grandpa wheeled over to me and
smiled. "When I was their age, I had to
fight villains on the way to school."

"That was then, this is now," Mom said.

"Well, at least we're all grounded together." Grandpa nudged me. "Now, how about some TV and ice cream?"

Mom walked Felicia and Gavin upstairs while they desperately tried to get out of the grounding. I think I heard Felicia try to bribe Mom with money. Dad went to his office to watch video footage of his battle with the Nefarious Brain and the robot raiders. He liked looking for ways to improve and stuff. I sat on the couch for a minute and thought about everything.

We weren't a perfect family by any means, but we were pretty darn special.

CHAPTER FOURTEEN
Weirdos

"I have an idea," I said to Chloe and Sandro. I'd felt empowered ever since I had stopped the Nefarious Brain, and there was something I wanted to try. I shared the plan with my friends. If we worked together, we could take down the new school bully. "We've got to hit Zack with everything we've got. And I mean EVERYTHING. But we have to work together."

Sandro shook his head. "You don't know how hard this is going to be for me. He took my candy bar *and* gave me a black eye," he explained. "Those two things are NOT COOL."

"I totally understand where you're coming from," I said. "But we have to try."

"You're right," Sandro said. "LET'S DO IT!"

Chloe nodded. "I'm in too."

We were going through with it. There was no turning back. Next time Zack came snooping around for trouble, we would be ready for him.

As if on cue, Zack showed up later that day. "What are you bore-bags up to? Other than being boring and ugly."

Sandro held out his candy bar to Zack.

"I give this candy bar to you freely in the hopes that you will appreciate its deliciousness the same way I do," he said. Zack took the candy bar and put it in his pocket. Phase 1: Complete. It was time for Chloe to do her thing.

"If you want some help with science homework this week, let me know. I can explain stuff to you and help you study for the quiz," offered Chloe.

Zack squinted in confusion. Phase 2: Mostly a success. Now, on to Peter Powers for the win!

"Want to join us for lunch?" I asked. "We can talk about whatever you want to talk about. That way, we can all get to know one another better."

Zack looked the three of us up and down. "Why are you guys being so nice, when I've been so awful?"

All three of us just smiled.

"I'm out of here. You guys are a bunch

of weirdos," he said. "But I'm keeping this candy bar…"

A few feet away, he stopped and whispered, "…and I will honor it with every bite." Then he walked away.

I put my arms around Sandro and Chloe. "YOU GUYS," I said. "That was some pretty sweet teamwork."

Sandro was fidgeting. "I'm going to miss that candy bar. Dark chocolate is expensive! But if it can change just one life, it's worth it."

"That was awesome," Chloe said. "But the joke's on him—I'm terrible at science. If he calls in that favor, he's in major trouble." We all laughed.

I've got the best friends in the world. Too bad I'm too grounded to hang with them outside of school.

CHAPTER FIFTEEN
A Happy Breakfast

Gavin, Felicia, and I had been up since six o'clock making breakfast for our parents. Well, *I* had been up since six o'clock making breakfast for our parents. My brother and sister were up too, but mostly complaining about my latest plan.

After I set the table and started making pancakes, Gavin finally began helping. Well, not Gavin, but his copies, Gavin #2 and Gavin #3. They scrambled some eggs and fried bacon while I did everything else. Gavin and Felicia were sitting at the table, waiting for breakfast to be done. It was kind of teamwork—thanks to the Gavin copies. At least they contributed *something*. That was enough for me.

The bacon was crisping, the potatoes were browning, and the flapjacks were flapping. Everything looked perfect.

"This better work," Felicia said. "I'm sick of being grounded."

"Yeah, I have plans this weekend. Big plans," Gavin said. "I can't be tied down to this place."

My siblings acted like our house was a prison. I didn't like being grounded, but it wasn't so bad hanging out with our family.

"Just relax and trust me," I assured Felicia and Gavin, carefully pouring fresh juice into every glass. "Making this breakfast for Mom and Dad will totally get us out of being grounded."

"Is that so?" Mom asked, strolling into the room casually. She was up earlier than I

expected. Ben must have been fussing.
"Tell me more about your plan."

Dad followed behind with Ben. "What
are you three doing up so early?" he
asked. "Smells good in here."

"They're making us breakfast so we'll
*un*ground them," Mom replied. She looked
over at Gavin and Felicia, who'd fallen back

asleep in their chairs and were snoring.
"Well, *Peter* is making us breakfast."

"With teamwork!" I half-smiled. As my
parents sat down to eat, I decided to come
clean about something that had been on
my mind. "Mom, I told you a fib."

"When?" she asked.

"Remember how I told you my class
presentation went *fine*? That wasn't exactly
true. You see, this bully at school actually
destroyed the whole thing. He's a new kid
and he's been giving me and my friends a
really hard time."

"Peter, do you need Mom and me to
come to school and talk to your teachers
about this?" asked Dad.

"No," I said. "Chloe, Sandro, and I decided the best thing we could do is smother him with kindness. He might be having a tough time himself, after all. Anyway, I'm sorry for lying about the presentation."

"I wish you'd told me the truth," Mom said. "But Dad and I are proud of you for treating this other boy the way you did, Peter. You can't shake hands with a clenched fist."

This was my chance, and I had to take it!

"So can I be ungrounded to go see *Vampire Boat* with Chloe and Sandro? I'll do extra chores for a week! Please, can I?" I asked. I was on pins and needles waiting for the reply.

"Of course not. You're grounded," Dad said matter-of-factly. FAIL. And I thought I was being so smooth. "But I like the way you handled yourself. You showed true leadership and teamwork—both in fighting the Brain and with this school bully. I think maybe we should talk about designing you a hero uniform. You won't be getting one for a while, but it couldn't hurt to start thinking about it."

"Seriously?!" I asked.

"Absolutely," Mom said. "We're proud of you."

YES! The incredible Peter Powers was back in the game. One day I was going to be a total superhero. Sure, I wasn't going to see a movie with my friends, but I'd be

ungrounded in no time...right?

A boy whose superpowers are
a little different from the rest...

LITTLE, BROWN AND COMPANY
BOOKS FOR YOUNG READERS

lb-kids.com

BOB797